Once You've
FEAR STREET . . .
Nothing Else Can Scare You.

People say Fear Street is the scariest place anywhere. They have seen ghosts in the Fear Street Cemetery, monsters in the Fear Street Woods, and strange creatures rising from the depths of Fear Lake.

Kelsey Moore has lived on Fear Street all her life. Nothing scares her. So when she and her cousin Drew encounter the strange fortuneteller Madame Valda, Kelsey just laughs. Even when Madame Valda tells Kelsey she has much to fear. But Kelsey isn't laughing when she climbs into bed—and finds it full of sand crabs. Or when she goes for a swim—and finds the ocean full of jellyfish.

Has Madame Valda doomed Kelsey to a life of fear? Read on to find out.

That is . . . if you're not afraid.

Also from R. L. Stine:

The Beast
The Beast 2

R. L. Stine's Ghosts of Fear Street
  #1 Hide and Shriek
  #2 Who's Been Sleeping in My Grave?
  #3 Attack of the Aqua Apes
  #4 Nightmare in 3-D
  #5 Stay Away from the Tree House

Available from MINSTREL Books

R·L·STINE'S
GHOSTS of FEAR STREET ®

EYE OF THE
FORTUNETELLER

A Parachute Press Book

A
MINSTREL®
BOOK

PUBLISHED BY POCKET BOOKS

New York   London   Toronto   Sydney   Tokyo   Singapore

This book is a work of fiction. Names, characters, places and incidents are products of the author's imagination or are used fictitiously. Any resemblance to actual events or locales or persons, living or dead, is entirely coincidental.

A MINSTREL PAPERBACK *Original*

 A Minstrel Paperback published by
POCKET BOOKS, a division of Simon & Schuster Inc.
1230 Avenue of the Americas, New York, NY 10020

Copyright © 1996 by Parachute Press, Inc.

EYE OF THE FORTUNETELLER WRITTEN BY A. G. CASCONE

ISBN: 0-671-52946-3

First Minstrel Books printing March 1996

10 9 8 7 6 5 4 3 2 1

FEAR STREET is a registered trademark of
Parachute Press, Inc.

A MINSTREL BOOK and colophon are registered trademarks
of Simon & Schuster Inc.

Cover art by Broeck Steadman

Printed in the U.S.A.

EYE OF THE
FORTUNETELLER

1

Kelsey Moore tried to scream, but the scream stuck in her throat. The giant Sea Serpent whipped her from side to side. It moved so fast that she could barely hold on. And then the green monster began to dive.

Kelsey tightened her grip. The Sea Serpent plunged down. Down. Down.

Kelsey screamed.

She screamed as the Sea Serpent, the biggest, wildest roller coaster at the beach, rounded the last corner and suddenly jerked to a stop.

"Wow!" Drew gasped. "I'm glad that's over."

"What a gyp," Kelsey said as she and Drew climbed

out of their seats. "I can't believe we stood in line for twenty minutes for that. It wasn't scary at all."

"A gyp!" Drew cried. "Are you crazy? It was totally scary."

"No, it wasn't," Kelsey said as they headed for the exit. "Did you ever ride the Exterminator at Echo Ridge? *That's* a scary ride."

"If it wasn't scary, how come you were screaming?" Drew asked.

"Me? Screaming?" Kelsey laughed. *"You* were the one who was screaming."

"I was not," Drew lied.

"Were, too," Kelsey replied. "The same way you screamed on the merry-go-round."

"Very funny," Drew shot back. "I screamed on the merry-go-round when we were six years old."

"Yeah, I know," Kelsey said. "It scared you so much, you haven't been on it since."

Drew reached out and yanked Kelsey's ponytail.

"Cut it out!" she yelled. But she wasn't really angry. Kelsey and Drew were best friends—and cousins. Cousins who looked practically liked twins.

They both had the same curly blond hair, the same freckles, the same green eyes. They even had the same last name. And they were the same age, too. Twelve. But Kelsey liked to brag that she was older—even if it was only by three weeks.

Every year their parents rented a house together at

the beach. And every year Kelsey had to drag Drew on all the rides. She loved them. He hated them.

It had taken Kelsey two whole summers to convince Drew to ride the Sea Serpent. And after all that, it was a total letdown.

"I'm telling you," Kelsey said. "I've had scarier walks to school."

"I know. I know. You live on Fear Street. There are ghosts and monsters there every day," Drew replied.

"The stories about Fear Street are true," Kelsey insisted. "Really strange things happen to people who live there."

"Nothing weird has happened to you," Drew pointed out.

"Not yet," Kelsey said. But she had plenty of stories to tell about the ghosts that haunted her neighborhood. And she told them to Drew about twice a day.

Drew rolled his eyes. "Okay. You're from Fear Street. Nothing scares you. Nothing except sand crabs."

"They don't scare me," Kelsey lied. "I just think they're gross, that's all. So what do you want to do now?" she asked, changing the subject.

"Go on the bumper cars?" Drew suggested.

"We can't," Kelsey replied. "We don't have enough money left."

"What are you talking about?" Drew started digging through his pockets. "We had almost ten dollars each."

"Drew, we've been on about a hundred rides," Kelsey began. And we spent a fortune trying to win that stupid prize you wanted."

"It's not stupid," Drew insisted. "That video game costs eighty bucks in the store. We could win it down here for only a quarter."

"If we could win it for a quarter, how come we've already spent *fifty* of them trying to get it? Besides, there's no way to win anything on those giant wheel games. They're rigged."

"That's not what you said last year," Drew reminded her. "Remember when you made us spend all our money trying to win that pink baby elephant?"

"Oh, yeah," Kelsey replied. "I remember—we didn't win one single game."

"Well, this time it's going to be different. This time we're going to win that video game," Drew declared.

"Okay, okay," Kelsey gave in. "But we should head home now. It's almost time for dinner. We'll try to win it tomorrow—when we can get more money."

Kelsey and Drew headed toward the part of the boardwalk that led to the exit.

"I have a little change left," Drew said, still searching through his pockets. "Let's buy some saltwater taffy—" Drew turned to Kelsey, but she was gone.

"Kelsey?"

"Over here," she called from around a corner. "Check this out."

"What is it?" Drew asked, turning the bend.

Kelsey stood in front of a creepy old shack. It was made of wood. Splintered, rotted wood that smelled ancient and moldy.

The small building sagged—the right side stood higher than the left. Kelsey tried to peer through one of the grimy windows, but it was covered with thick iron bars. Heavy black curtains draped the panes.

"I don't know what this is," Kelsey said, circling the strange old shack. "I've never seen it before."

Kelsey glanced up and spotted a sign that hung over the doorway. *"The Amazing Zandra,"* she read, trying to sound spooky. "It's a stupid gypsy fortune-telling place—only the Amazing Zandra is 'Out to Lunch.'" Kelsey pointed to the sign.

Drew pressed his nose up against the window in the door to peek inside. He leaped back, crashing into Kelsey.

"Ouch!" she cried out, rubbing her foot. "What's the matter with you?"

5

"Take a look," Drew whispered.

Kelsey pressed her nose up against the dirty window. She peered into the dark room. Squinting.

Then she saw it.

A skeleton.

A human skeleton. It stared at her with its hollow eyes.

She inhaled sharply. Then laughed.

"It's just a skeleton. A prop," she told Drew. "Fortunetellers use stuff like that all the time. To make you think they're spooky and mysterious."

Kelsey jiggled the doorknob. The door opened with a loud click. "Let's go in!"

"No way," Drew told her, stepping back from the door. "We don't have time. We'll be late for dinner."

"You're such a chicken," Kelsey taunted.

"I am not," Drew shot back. "There's just no reason to go in. Fortunetellers are fakes. Everyone knows that. They can't really tell the future."

Kelsey pulled the door open wide enough to stick her head inside. The air inside the shack felt icy cold. It sent a chill down her spine.

She glanced around the room. A layer of thick dust carpeted the floor. Old books were scattered everywhere.

Kelsey's gaze shifted to the far wall of the shack,

where bookshelves rose from the floor to the ceiling. On them sat tons and tons of stuffed animals.

Kelsey stared at the animals. They weren't like the ones she had in her room.

These were real animals.

Real dead animals.

"You're not going to believe what's in here," Kelsey whispered. "Let's go in."

"No way!" Drew repeated. Then he tugged Kelsey back. "Let's go. We'll be here all summer. We can come back another time."

Kelsey sighed. "Oh, all right, but—"

"Stay. Stay," a raspy voice called from the back of the shack.

Kelsey and Drew turned in time to see a very old woman make her way to the front of the shack. She pointed a wrinkled, gnarled finger at them. "Come," she said. "Come in."

Kelsey stared at the woman. She wore a red flowered dress that hung down to the floor. Her face was lined with wrinkles. And her mouth twisted in a half sneer. But it was her earrings that Kelsey gaped at.

Dozens of gold rings dangled from each ear. Heavy gold earrings that pulled on her lobes and made them hang low.

She fixed her dark eyes on Kelsey as she spoke again.

Kelsey gasped. The woman had one blue eye and one eye the color of coal.

"Come," the woman beckoned. "Come inside. There is much to tell. Come, Kelsey and Drew."

All the color drained from Drew's face. "Kelsey, how does she know our names?" he murmured. "How does she know?"

2

"**S**he probably heard us talking," Kelsey whispered to Drew.

"But we just walked around the shack. She wasn't there," he replied.

"Maybe she heard us through the windows or something," Kelsey answered. "Trust me, these fortunetellers are all fakes. You said so yourself."

"Come, children," the gypsy woman continued, opening the door wider. "Come inside." Then she gazed over her shoulder. "I have something for you."

"Um, thanks. But we can't," Drew said. "We really have to get home."

The gypsy ignored him. And so did Kelsey. She

9

followed the old woman inside. Drew lunged for Kelsey's arm and tried to pull her back, but Kelsey jerked free.

"You have some pretty neat things in here," Kelsey said to the woman as she stepped inside.

"These are not my things," she replied. Then she sat down behind a round table. "Sit." She motioned to two chairs. "You may call me Madame Valda."

"I thought she was supposed to be the Amazing Zandra," Drew whispered as the two took their seats at the table.

Kelsey shrugged as she watched the gypsy set a folded velvet cloth on the table in front of her. It was bloodred and held something inside it.

"Madame Valda will tell your fortune now," the gypsy announced. Then she opened the cloth to reveal a deck of cards.

"But we don't have any money to pay you, uh, Madame Gypsy," Drew said, standing.

"Madame Valda," the old woman corrected sharply. "I will do it for nothing," her voice softened. "Sit! It is a great honor to have Madame Valda tell your fortune."

"Sit!" Kelsey echoed.

Drew sat. Madame Valda spread the deck of cards out on the table. She began to sing softly in a language Kelsey had never heard.

Kelsey watched as the fortuneteller swirled her head around in a circle. She'd seen fortunetellers in the movies do this. They closed their eyes and sang themselves into some kind of trance.

Only Madame Valda wasn't closing her eyes.

She stared straight ahead. Straight at Kelsey.

This is really creepy, Kelsey thought. A nervous giggle escaped her lips.

Madame Valda didn't seem to notice—or she didn't care.

She continued to sing.

She continued to stare.

Directly into Kelsey's eyes.

Kelsey stared back. She felt as if she were in some kind of trance, too. She couldn't stop gazing into the woman's weird eyes.

Finally Madame Valda's chant came to an end, and she shifted her gaze to the deck of cards on the table.

Kelsey let out a long sigh. She didn't realize she'd been holding her breath.

Madame Valda flipped over three cards. They all had strange symbols on them. Symbols that Kelsey had never seen before.

The gypsy studied the cards for a moment, then turned to Drew.

"Drew Moore," she said. "I see that you are sometimes more a follower than a leader. You must be

11

careful to guard against that. It will get you into trouble. Especially when you let Kelsey make all the decisions."

Kelsey shot a quick glance at Drew. His jaw dropped and his eyes grew wide.

Kelsey squirmed in her chair. *How did she know Drew's last name?* she wondered. *How?* Kelsey knew she never said it. And neither did Drew. Not outside. And not inside.

Then she spotted it. Drew's beach pass. Pinned to his shirt. With his name printed in big red letters, Drew T. Moore. Kelsey laughed out loud as she stared down at her own badge. Then she pointed it out to Drew.

"What is funny?" The old woman snarled.

"Um. Nothing," Kelsey replied.

"Then why do you laugh?" the old woman pressed.

"Well, it's just that your fortunetelling powers aren't all that, um, mysterious," Kelsey confessed.

Drew kicked Kelsey under the table.

"Do you think Madame Valda is a fake?" The old woman's voice rose to a screech.

"I *know* Madame Valda is a fake," Kelsey replied, imitating the gypsy's accent.

"You have insulted the famous Madame Valda," the fortuneteller roared. She jerked to her feet and loomed over Kelsey. "Apologize now, or live the rest of your life in fear."

"In fear of what?" Kelsey asked, staring directly into Madame Valda's dark eye. "I'm not afraid of you."

"Oh, yes, you are!" Madame Valda cried. "I am the most powerful fortuneteller who ever lived. And I know all your fears, you foolish child. All your fears!"

"Just say you're sorry and let's go," Drew said, pushing his chair from the table. Then he added in a whisper, "She's worse than scary—she's nuts."

"No," Kelsey told Drew. "I am *not* afraid."

Madame Valda's eyes flickered. She leaned in, closer to Kelsey. Kelsey could feel the gypsy's hot breath on her face. Then she whispered, "Only a fool is not afraid."

Before Kelsey could reply, the old woman reached down and flipped over the next card in the deck. She threw it down onto the table in front of Kelsey.

It looked like a joker.

Kelsey read the words on the bottom of the card— the Fool.

"The cards never lie! You are the fool, and I curse you for the rest of your life. Now get out!" she cried. "Get out. Now!"

Kelsey and Drew jumped up and bolted for the door. Madame Valda's voice thundered behind them. "You will believe. You will know *fear.*"

As soon as Kelsey's and Drew's feet hit the board-walk, they broke into a run.

But Madame Valda's voice trailed after them. "Fear! Fear! Fear!" she cried out over their pounding sneakers. "You will know fear!"

Kelsey and Drew ran faster. But Madame Valda's voice seemed as close as before. Kelsey glanced back. "Oh, no!" she cried. "She is crazy! She's coming after us!"

3

Kelsey's heart pounded as she ran faster.

Her lungs felt as if they were about to explode.

She turned back—and there was Madame Valda. Right behind her!

This is unreal, Kelsey's mind whirled. How could an old lady run so fast?

"She's right behind us!" Drew cried out, panting.

"Leave us alone!" Kelsey screamed over her shoulder.

Madame Valda's right eye burned into Kelsey— and Kelsey stopped running.

"Run! Run!" Drew screamed.

But Kelsey couldn't move. She felt paralyzed. Frozen in place by the dark eye of the fortuneteller.

The gypsy reached out and clutched Kelsey's shoulder with her bony fingers. A sharp pain shot down Kelsey's arm. She tried to jerk away, but Madame Valda held her tightly.

The old gypsy laughed. A hideous laugh.

"Not afraid!" she cackled. "Oh, yes. You will be afraid!" She whisked the Fool card before Kelsey's eyes, then tossed it in the air.

"Fool! Fool! Fool!" she cried. "Only a fool is not afraid!"

Kelsey and Drew watched as the card flew up. And up. And up. Until it faded to a white flicker in the sky. Then it was gone.

Kelsey wrenched free of Madame Valda's grip, and she and Drew flew down the boardwalk. She ran so fast, her lungs burned in her chest. She quickly glanced back—to see if the fortuneteller was still following them.

But Madame Valda was gone.

"Drew! Stop!" Kelsey grabbed her cousin's arm. "Look! Madame Valda. She disappeared."

Drew spun around. Kelsey was right. Madame Valda had simply vanished.

"How did she run so fast?" Drew asked, out of breath.

"I don't know," Kelsey replied, shaking her head. "Do you think she really was a fortuneteller? I mean, a *real* fortuneteller? With *real* powers?"

"Come on, Kelsey," Drew replied. "Now you sound as crazy as that old hag."

"Yeah, you're right," Kelsey said. But she didn't sound as if she meant it. "So, um, you don't think she put a curse on us, right?" Kelsey asked.

"Not on me," Drew answered. "I was nice to her, remember?"

"Thanks a lot." Kelsey punched Drew in the arm.

"Come on, Kelsey," Drew said. "She probably isn't even a real gypsy."

Kelsey knew that Drew was probably right. But she kept picturing the fortuneteller's strange eyes. And she kept hearing her voice. That horrible voice screaming, "Fool! Fool! Fool!"

"Forget the fortuneteller." Drew headed toward the exit. "We've got real problems. We're late for dinner."

Kelsey checked her watch. "Oh, no!" she groaned. "We're already a half hour late. Mom's going to kill us!"

Kelsey and Drew hurried out the exit. They were only eight blocks from the beach house. If they ran, they'd be home in five minutes.

"Let's take the shortcut home," Kelsey suggested as she dashed ahead of Drew. "It's right there." She pointed ahead. "The alley that runs behind the Italian restaurant."

Drew followed Kelsey past the restaurant and into the narrow, winding alley.

"Where does this go?" Drew asked as they sprinted around the alley's turns and curves.

"To the parking lot on Eighteenth Street," Kelsey answered. "Then we'll be only two blocks from home."

But as they rounded the last curve, Kelsey knew something was wrong. She faced a dead end—a sooty brick wall that rose at least twenty feet high. No parking lot.

"This is really strange," she said, glancing around the alley. It was dark and dingy. Totally deserted. "I'm sure there was a parking lot here last summer."

"Maybe they bricked it up during the winter," Drew suggested. "Let's just get out of here."

Kelsey started back the way they came. Drew followed. But when they reached the other end of the alley—nothing looked the same! Even the Italian restaurant was gone.

Kelsey eyes darted left and right.

"Hey! What's going on?" she cried. "This is so weird. Where are we?"

"I don't know," Drew answered, searching for a street sign. "This has to be the way we came in."

"The restaurant was right on this corner," Kelsey said. "I know it was."

Kelsey stared at the spot where the restaurant should have been. In its place stood an old shingled house with boarded-up windows.

"I don't get it," she mumbled to herself. She'd been coming to this town practically forever. She knew every square inch of it. But suddenly she had no idea where she was.

She glanced around. The alley now led into a street. When Kelsey looked down the street, she noticed a few rundown shacks. Nothing more. In the other direction the street was dark and gloomy and lined with battered houses and abandoned storefronts.

"All right," Kelsey said, trying to stay calm. "The beach must be that way." She pointed to her right. "So that means our house must be this way." Kelsey motioned to the gloomy street.

"That way?" Drew gasped. "I've never even seen that street before. It's totally creepy. We're not going down there."

"I'm telling you, that's the way we have to go," Kelsey insisted and began jogging down the dreary block. "Come on!"

Drew followed her for about three blocks—until she stopped.

"Wait," Kelsey said, out of breath. "This can't be right."

"I told you this wasn't the way to go," Drew muttered. "There aren't any creepy old buildings like these anywhere near our house."

"I know. I know," Kelsey replied. "We'd better ask somebody for directions."

"Like who?" Drew asked.

Good question, Kelsey realized. She gazed up and down the street. There was no one to ask. She and Drew were all alone.

"Where is everybody anyway?" Drew asked. "There should be tons of people everywhere—we're right by the beach."

"The beach," Kelsey repeated. "That's it. We should head for the beach. Then we'll be able to find our way home."

Before Drew could reply, Kelsey took off down a side street. A street she was certain headed toward the shore. But when she reached the next corner, her heart sank.

Nothing but shabby houses. Gutted storefronts. Every way she turned.

No people. No beach.

Kelsey was beginning to think that she and Drew would be lost forever. Tiny beads of sweat formed on her forehead. She wiped them away with the back of her hand.

"This is getting really scary," Drew said when he caught up to her. He glanced down and kicked a jagged piece of glass on the sidewalk.

"What was that?" Kelsey jumped back.

"Just a broken piece of glass," Drew answered.

"No. That—listen," Kelsey replied.

A dog.

Kelsey caught sight of it first.

A big, mangy yellow dog.

She gasped. It was the biggest dog she had ever seen. And it was headed straight for them.

"Let's get out of here!" she screamed.

They crossed the street and charged ahead, but the dog ran faster. Gaining on them. Its wild barks echoed in Kelsey's ears.

Kelsey and Drew stopped on the next corner to catch their breath. They ducked into a darkened doorway, pressing their backs against the door's iron gate. Gasping for air.

They listened.

Silence.

"Do you think it's gone?" Drew asked.

"I-I don't know," Kelsey stammered. "I'll check." She poked her head out from their hiding place.

A pair of crazed yellowed eyes met hers.

The dog sat on its haunches—just a few feet away. It growled. A low growl that exposed two decayed fangs—dripping with saliva.

"Run!" Kelsey cried, grabbing Drew's hand.

The two bolted from the doorway. They flew down the street, holding hands, with Kelsey in the lead.

Kelsey glanced behind her. The dog tore after them. Howling now. And snapping its jaws hungrily.

Kelsey turned down a narrow alleyway. It looked just like the first alley. Only darker. Much darker. And the farther they ran, the narrower it grew.

They dodged around splintered pieces of wood. Shards of glass.

The wild beast charged up behind them, snarling. Its wet, gray tongue hung from its mouth. Kelsey could almost feel the animal's sharp teeth sink into her ankles.

"Faster!" she screamed. "Run faster!"

With a burst of speed the two raced ahead, leaving the dog a few yards behind.

The alley curved sharply to the right. Drew nearly stumbled as the two took the turn.

And then Kelsey stopped. What lay ahead of her was suddenly as terrifying as the wild dog behind her.

Another dead end.

There was no way out.

"We're trapped!" Kelsey shrieked. "We're trapped!"

4

Kelsey and Drew pressed their backs against the building. Waiting. Waiting for the vicious dog to appear.

Kelsey held her breath and listened.

No barking. No snarling.

"Maybe we lost him," she whispered.

"I don't think so," Drew whispered back.

Kelsey silently agreed. The alley went only one way. That dog would have to be pretty stupid to lose track of us, she thought.

"But why isn't he attacking?" she asked Drew.

"I don't know," he replied, shaking his head.

The two waited in silence. The blood pounded in Kelsey's head.

Another minute passed—the longest minute in Kelsey's life—with no sign of the dog. "We can't just stand here, Drew," Kelsey said, finally breaking the quiet. "I'm going to check."

Kelsey tiptoed to the curve in the alley. She peeked around the corner. Slowly.

The alley stood deserted.

No dog.

"It's gone!" Kelsey gasped.

"This is so weird," Drew replied, making his way to her side. "How could it just disappear like that?"

"I don't know. And I don't care. Let's get out of here. Now," Kelsey answered. "Um, you go first."

"Gee, thanks a lot," Drew said as he started down the alley.

They walked quickly but carefully.

Listening.

Listening for any sign of the deadly beast. But the only sound they heard was the soft thumping of their own feet.

The alley seemed even darker than before. And for the first time Kelsey noticed how sour it smelled. The stench flooded her nostrils and made her sick.

"Look!" Drew exclaimed. He stopped short, and Kelsey slammed into him.

"What?" she asked. Her heart skipped a beat. She was afraid to hear the answer.

"I can't believe it!" Drew shouted. "Look where we are!"

Kelsey inched alongside Drew and peered out of the dark alleyway—into bright sunlight.

She knew immediately where she was. But she glanced up at the street sign for proof.

Thirteenth Street.

Less than a block away from their house.

"I thought we were totally lost," Drew said as he started toward their street. He let out a long sigh. "And all the time we were less than a block away from home. That's the last time I follow *you*," he added.

Kelsey was about to shoot back a smart remark of her own when she remembered something strange. Really strange.

"Drew, do you remember what the fortuneteller told you? You know, about getting into trouble if you follow me all the time? You don't think . . ."

A shiver of fear crept down Kelsey's spine. She stopped to glance back at the alleyway.

But it was gone!

You will believe. You will know fear. The fortuneteller's words echoed in Kelsey's mind.

I'm going crazy, Kelsey thought. The alley is there. It must be there. I probably can't see it from this angle—that's all.

"Come on, Kelsey," Drew called. "We're really late!"

25

Kelsey broke into a run. The two raced the rest of the way home. As they neared their house, they spotted their parents sitting outside on the front porch.

"Where have you been?" Kelsey's mother asked.

"Do you know how late it is?" Drew's mother added.

"Sorry," Kelsey apologized. "We got . . ." She was about to say lost, but she stopped herself. If she told them they were lost, she knew what would happen. Their parents would never allow them to go out by themselves anymore. "We were having so much fun on the boardwalk, we lost track of the time."

"We won't do it again," Drew added. "We promise."

"All right." Her mother forgave her more quickly than she ever did at home.

That was one of the best things about being on vacation. Parents were so much easier to get along with.

"Come inside and wash your hands for dinner," Drew's mother instructed. Then their parents led the way inside.

As Kelsey climbed the porch steps, she thought about the old fortuneteller again. Now that she was safe at home, the whole thing seemed pretty dumb.

"Fool!" Kelsey heard the echo of the old gypsy woman's voice. Only this time she started to laugh at herself—for acting like one.

Kelsey was about to step through the front door when something caught her eye. Something falling from the sky. Fluttering. Fluttering. Down. Down. Down.

Drew spotted it, too. "What is that?" he asked, squinting as he gazed up.

"I can't tell," Kelsey replied, watching the object float down on a breeze.

And then it landed right at Kelsey's feet.

She gasped.

It was the card.

The card that the old gypsy woman had tossed into the air.

Kelsey trembled as she stared at it. As she stared down into the face of the Fool.

5

That night Kelsey sat on her bed, alone in her room, staring at the Fool card.

"*You* are the Fool, Madame Whatever-your-name-is," Kelsey muttered. "And you are *not* going to scare me. No way."

Kelsey turned the card over and over in her hand. Then she ripped it in half. Then ripped it in half again. And again. "So there!" she declared when she was through.

She scooped up every last bit of paper and dumped it all into the wastepaper basket near her dresser.

"Tomorrow will be a much better day," she promised herself as she slipped between the sheets. Then she closed her eyes.

She pictured herself at the beach with Drew. They would spend the whole day there, she decided. Swimming in the ocean. Collecting shells. Playing volleyball. Lying in the sun.

Kelsey could imagine the warmth of the sun on her skin as she snuggled into her pillow. It felt good—even in her imagination.

Then she started to drift off to sleep—pretending that she was already on the beach.

But something tickled her left foot. She rubbed at it with her right one.

But the tickle returned.

Now it moved up the back of her leg.

Kelsey brushed her leg against the sheet. But it didn't work. The tickle kept moving—moving up her leg.

Only now it wasn't a tickle. It felt prickly.

Kelsey brushed her leg with her foot. But the prickly feeling didn't go away.

It started to spread.

Over her legs. Her arms. Her whole body.

She tried to ignore it.

She fluffed her pillow and rolled over on her side. But that didn't work, either.

Now it felt as though her whole bed had come alive. With tiny little legs.

Millions of them.

Skittering across her body.

29

Crawling into her hair. Stinging her skin.

She shot up in bed. She stared at the sheets. At her body. But it was too dark to see.

And then she felt it.

A tiny set of legs creeping across her cheek.

And she knew what it was.

Sand crabs! Even in the dark, she knew. She hated sand crabs—they terrified her!

She shrieked with horror.

Her hands flew to her legs. Her arms. Her face. Frantically trying to brush the creatures away.

"Get off!" she cried. "Get off!"

But within seconds they swarmed over her entire body.

Kelsey grew frightened. So frightened that she couldn't breathe.

She tried to scream. But all that came out was a choked whimper—as she felt one of the disgusting little creatures start to crawl inside her ear.

6

Kelsey leaped out of bed.

She threw her head from side to side. "Get out!" she screamed. "Get out!"

The stinging in her ear stopped. But her hair felt alive. Alive with the horrible creatures.

She scratched her head. Scratched until her scalp turned raw.

She had to look in the mirror. She had to see the crabs. To see where they were. To get them off.

She flipped on the light switch and headed for the mirror over her dresser. She didn't want to look. She didn't want to see those disgusting crabs—with their hideous pincers creeping on her skin.

But she forced herself to look.

And then she screamed.

No sand crabs.

Not in her hair. Not on her face.

Nowhere.

She spun around to face her bed—expecting to see it crawling with sand crabs.

Nothing there, either. Nothing but her clean blue sheets and plump white pillow.

Kelsey quickly pulled back the cover. No creatures hiding anywhere.

What is going on? she wondered. *What is wrong with me?* She glanced over at her clock—2:00 A.M. Suddenly she felt exhausted.

She checked her bed once more before dropping into it. But she couldn't fall asleep. Her skin still felt tingly. Still felt as if thousands of tiny legs were creeping all over it.

She thought about the creatures. She pictured them swarming all over her body. A low groan escaped her lips.

What if they come back? She shuddered.

She propped up her pillows and decided to stay up all night. But she was tired. So tired. And before she knew it, she drifted off to sleep.

The early dawn light fell upon Kelsey's face and woke her up. She turned over her pillow and tried to fall back asleep—but she heard something. Something nearby.

Her eyes popped open and searched the room.

There it was.

On the floor.

A sand crab. A single sand crab.

Kelsey watched in horror as it skittered across her floor and darted under her bed.

Oh, no! She gasped. What if there were millions of sand crabs. Millions of them under her bed. Waiting for her.

Her heart pounded in her chest. Her temples throbbed. But she knew she had to look. She had to know.

Kelsey checked the floor carefully before she slid out of bed. Then she kneeled down and peered underneath the bed, into the darkness.

She spotted her slippers. An old *Teen* magazine. And a lot of dust.

Then she saw it.

Not the sand crab. Not even a thousand sand crabs. It was something much more horrible.

Kelsey's lower lip trembled. Her hands began to shake.

She squeezed her eyes shut, hoping that when she opened them, the terrible thing would be gone. Just the way all those sand crabs had disappeared.

But when she opened her eyes, it was still there.

The Fool card that she had ripped to shreds.

There it was.

Under her bed.

All in one piece.

A ray of sunlight filtered through her window and fell upon the card. And Kelsey could see the Fool's menacing grin—the menacing grin that was meant just for her.

7

"**S**o were the crabs real or not?" Drew asked.

Kelsey told Drew all about her terrible night as the two walked to the beach the next morning.

"I told you!" Kelsey yelled. "They weren't real. Well, one of them was real. But not the others."

"So—why were you afraid?"

"Look!" Kelsey said, shoving the Fool card right in his face.

"So?" Drew pushed her hand away.

"So!" Kelsey couldn't believe that he could be so dumb. "I told you. I tore it up into a million pieces and threw it into the garbage can! Now look at this thing. It isn't even bent or creased."

"This just doesn't make any sense," Drew said as

35

they reached the beach and started tromping through the sand.

"Wow, Drew. When did you become such a genius?"

"Very funny," Drew grumbled. "So—what are you going to do?"

"Well, I am definitely not going to let that old gypsy and her stupid curse scare me," Kelsey declared. "And now I am going to get rid of this card—forever."

Kelsey headed directly to the ocean. She stood on the shore for a few moments and watched the waves roll in.

"What are you doing?" Drew asked.

"Watch," she told him. She held up the Fool card and tore it again and again and again—until she couldn't tear it anymore.

Then, with Drew by her side, she waded out into the water. When the first wave broke around her knees, she scattered some of the bits of paper over the water.

She and Drew watched as the foam carried them away.

When the next wave hit, she did the same thing, scattering a little more of what was left of the card. Wave after wave, she did the same thing—until nothing was left.

"There," she said as the surf carried off the last torn pieces. "It's gone for good. Now let's go swimming."

"We have to wait for our parents," Drew reminded her. "You know the rules. 'No swimming, kids, unless we're with you.'"

"Yeah, yeah, I know. But they promised they were coming out right away," Kelsey complained. "Where are they anyway?"

She scanned the beach, searching for them. "There they are!" she said, spotting them.

Kelsey jumped up and down, waving at their parents to get their attention. When they waved back, Kelsey darted into the ocean.

"Race you to France," she called over her shoulder to Drew.

Drew dived in after her.

They fought their way through crashing waves until they were shoulder-deep in the water. Kelsey watched as a wave began to swell behind them.

"Let's ride this one," she yelled.

"All right!" Drew yelled back.

Kelsey bent her knees and pushed off the sandy floor. Drew did the same. The wave took them on an awesome ride. Perfect all the way to the end.

They swam out and waited to catch the next wave. Suddenly Kelsey felt something squishy hit her back. And it stayed there—right between her shoulders.

"Drew," she called. "Do you see something on my back?"

But Drew wasn't there. He had caught the wave and was headed for the shore.

She reached over her shoulder to swat off whatever was there. The tips of her fingers brushed against something soft.

Something wet and slimy.

Something that began to wriggle against her skin.

"Jellyfish!" she shrieked in terror.

She tried to brush it off, but it wouldn't budge.

She jumped up and down and tried to shake it off. The more she struggled with it, the tighter it clung to her.

Digging into her back.

Stinging her with its deadly poison.

8

"**D**rew!" Kelsey screamed. "Drew! Help me!"

But Drew was riding his wave to the shore. He couldn't hear her.

Kelsey dug her nails into her back. Trying to scratch the jellyfish off. Her fingers sunk into its gooey body. And with a sickening *thwop,* it closed around her hand.

"Help me!" she screamed. "Somebody, help me!" She twisted and turned until she wrenched her hand free.

Get back to shore, she thought. *That's what I have to do!*

A wave began to swell. I'll ride it in, Kelsey decided. It will be the fastest way back.

As soon as it reached her, Kelsey pushed off and tried to catch it. But her timing was off, and she missed. She tried for the next one. But the wave seemed to wash right over her.

She missed wave after wave. And it seemed like the harder she tried, the faster the waves passed her by.

Her skin started to burn under the creature's slimy hold.

"Swim in!" she told herself. "Just get to shore and get help!"

Kelsey paddled as hard as she could. But she seemed to be moving in slow motion. She noticed that the water around her was churning. Growing thick and cloudy.

She swam harder. Her hands thrashed the water. But she felt as if she were swimming in Jell-O.

Why is it so hard to move? she wondered. Why am I stuck in the same spot?

The jellyfish on her back gripped her skin. A sharp pain shot through her body.

Kelsey kicked her legs. Harder and harder.

Her arms ached. And the muscles in her shins were beginning to cramp. With every move, she gasped for breath. But she had to get to shore. She had to get that jellyfish off her back.

I must be close to the beach now, Kelsey thought.

She looked up.

She was farther away than when she started!

"How can that be?" she screamed.

She needed to rest before she tried to make her way back again. She closed her eyes. Then she flipped over on her back and floated for a few seconds—until she felt something on her shoulders.

She turned her head from side to side.

Two blobs rested on her shoulders.

Two hideous bluish blobs.

Jellyfish!

Giant blue blobs of jellyfish!

The shiny blue blob that sucked on her right shoulder was chunky and clear. But the one on her left shoulder had little red lines running through it.

Poisonous! She was certain.

She flipped over quickly, but before she could peel the horrible creatures off, her legs began to sting. Then her arms. Then her stomach and the back of her neck. Even the soles of her feet.

"They're all over me!" she shrieked.

Some were small—like clear jellybeans. Others had tentacles that shimmered in the water. They curled around her limbs. Closing around them. Tighter and tighter.

A tiny one was stuck to Kelsey's eyelash. Every time she blinked, she looked through its slimy, cloudy body.

Kelsey's heart raced. She felt dizzy. Everything around her started to spin.

Don't panic! she told herself. *Swim!*

Kelsey's arms sliced through the water as she struggled toward the shore.

But swimming grew harder and harder.

The water felt thick and gooey.

She was swimming in a sea of jellyfish!

Kelsey's eyes darted around her. There were jellyfish everywhere. There seemed to be more jellyfish than water. Waves of jellyfish rolled toward her. Crashing against her skin with a sickening splat.

She flailed through the sea of slime. "I'm not going to make it," she groaned. "I'm not going to make it back."

The jellyfish sea thickened around her. She could barely lift her arms to swim anymore.

And then a huge wave lifted her up and carried her toward the shore. As soon as her foot hit the ocean's sandy bottom, she stood up and charged out of the water.

"Help me!" she screamed. "Somebody, help me get these things off!"

But the people on the beach didn't move.

Why wasn't anyone helping her? What was wrong with them?

"Kelsey!" Drew shouted. She spun around to face him. "What is wrong with you?"

"Jellyfish! Jellyfish!" was all Kelsey could say, shaking her stinging arms and legs.

"What jellyfish?" Drew asked, staring out into the ocean.

"The ones all over me!" Kelsey cried. "Look!"

"Kelsey," Drew replied, "there are no jellyfish on you."

9

Kelsey stared at her arms. She stretched out her legs and searched them. She ran her fingers through her hair.

No jellyfish.

"There *were* jellyfish," Kelsey insisted, rubbing the skin on her arms, trying to get rid of the slimy feeling she still had. "They were all over me! And the whole ocean was full of them!"

Kelsey noticed that the people all around them were listening to her—trying not to laugh.

"Do you see them now?" Drew asked.

Kelsey stared into the water. She and Drew stood there.

Silently.

Watching the water wash up around their feet.

Clean, clear water. Not a jellyfish in sight.

"No," Kelsey admitted. "But something really creepy is going on."

"I'll say," Drew agreed.

"You don't think I'm going nuts, do you?" she asked.

"Nah," he answered. "You're not *going* nuts. You *are* nuts."

"Ha, ha." Kelsey tried to smile.

Then she felt something hit her ankle. And she jumped away, practically knocking Drew over.

"Jellyfish!" she screamed before she could stop herself.

Drew looked down.

Kelsey saw his face freeze in horror.

"Is it a jellyfish?" she cried. "Is it?"

"No," Drew whispered. "Not a jellyfish."

Kelsey slowly glanced down. There, lying at her feet was the Fool card.

All in one piece.

Grinning up at her with its evil grin.

"M-maybe this is a different card," Drew stuttered.

Kelsey kneeled to pick it up. "Drew, I think that fortuneteller really did put a curse on me." She sighed. "I can't believe it. I spend my whole life living on Fear Street and nothing terrible happens to me.

45

But I come down to the shore for a week and I end up with a curse!"

"Look," Drew said nervously, "if you really have been cursed, there's got to be a way to get rid of it, right?"

"How am I supposed to know?" she shot back. "Do I look like a gypsy to you?"

"Well, maybe we should go find that weird old lady again," he started. "And maybe if you apologize to her, she'll take the curse off."

"She should apologize to me," Kelsey said. "She's ruining my vacation."

"Get real, Kelsey. We've got to do something."

"Okay, okay." Kelsey agreed. "Let's go find that stupid witch."

Kelsey told their parents that she and Drew were going to play some skeet ball at the arcade. Then they headed for the boardwalk to search for the old gypsy woman.

"What am I supposed to say when we find her?" Kelsey asked Drew. "I'm sorry I thought you were a fake—please take this curse off of me?"

"That sounds pretty good," Drew said as they headed down the boardwalk. "Look. Here's the pizza place. The shack should be right around this corner."

Kelsey followed Drew around the corner—and there it was. As Kelsey approached it, a horrible thought crossed her mind.

What if the gypsy refuses to remove the curse?
What would she do then?

"Are you ready?" Drew asked, walking up to the door.

Kelsey nodded.

Drew opened the door and Kelsey stepped inside.

The skeleton was still there. But now it seemed to be staring right at her. Following her every move.

Kelsey shivered.

Then from a darkened corner a voice called out, "Welcome." Kelsey stared at the figure. She sat at the table, staring into her crystal ball.

But something about her wasn't right.

"Welcome," the shadowed figure called again. Even though Kelsey couldn't see her face, she knew that it wasn't the same gypsy.

"The Amazing Zandra will tell your fortune," the woman continued, without any kind of accent at all.

When the Amazing Zandra finally glanced up, Kelsey could see that she wasn't nearly as spooky. Or nearly as old as the other gypsy.

In fact, the Amazing Zandra didn't look much older than Kelsey's next-door neighbor—who just started high school last year.

Kelsey even thought she was kind of pretty. Her wavy hair was long and brown. And her eyes were ordinary. Brown. Both of them.

Zandra's fingernails were painted purple. And she

had a ring on every finger. She wasn't nearly as mysterious or spooky as Madame Valda.

"I have to see the other gypsy," Kelsey announced.

"There is no other gypsy," Zandra informed them.

"Yes, there is," Drew said. "She was here yesterday. She's really old and wrinkly."

"You must be mistaken," Zandra insisted. "There is no other gypsy here. And there never has been."

Kelsey felt her heart sink.

"Oh, no," she moaned. "Now what am I going to do? I'm going to be cursed forever!"

10

"**A**re you sure there isn't another gypsy?" Drew asked again.

"Look, kid," Zandra replied. "I'm the gypsy who works here, okay? The only gypsy. Now do you want me to tell your fortune or not?"

The Amazing Zandra is lying to us, Kelsey thought. She has to be.

"Look, Amazing Zandra," Kelsey said as politely as she could. "We were here yesterday. But you weren't. There was a different gypsy. She was real, *real* old."

"And scary," Drew added.

But Zandra just kept shaking her head no.

"She had a really strange accent," Kelsey went on. Nothing. Just more head-shaking from Zandra.

49

"She put a curse on me," Kelsey said hopelessly.

With that, Zandra's expression changed. "A curse?" she gasped, clutching her heart. "If you are under the curse of a gypsy, you are in very serious trouble."

"Tell me about it," Kelsey said.

"Perhaps I *can* help you," the Amazing Zandra replied.

"Really?" Kelsey asked nervously.

"Yes, really," Zandra answered. "Only it isn't easy to remove a curse," she added. "And it isn't cheap, either."

"How much?" Kelsey asked Zandra.

"Ten dollars."

"Ten dollars!" Kelsey gasped.

That was a lot of money. It was all the money she had. She had planned to spend it on carnival games and rides and ice cream.

But she had no choice. She didn't know if Zandra was a real gypsy or not. But she was her only hope.

She handed the money over to the fortuneteller. "Take the curse off me," she told her.

"First you must explain to me exactly how you were cursed," Zandra said. "Did the old gypsy give the curse a name?"

"No," Kelsey said. "But she called me a name."

"And what was that?" Zandra asked.

"A fool," Kelsey told her. "And she got real mad at me for not believing in her."

Zandra shook her head gravely.

"Now all these terrible things are happening to me," Kelsey continued. "Yesterday, we got lost. And last night hundreds of sand crabs attacked me in my sleep."

"And this morning," Drew jumped in, "she thought she was smothered in jellyfish."

Zandra cringed.

"And no matter what I do," Kelsey went on, "I can't seem to get rid of this card." Kelsey placed the Fool card down on the table in front of Zandra.

"I've torn it up twice. But it just keeps coming back, right after something really bad happens to me."

"Ah," Zandra nodded knowingly. "The Fool Card Curse. This is a very powerful curse," she told Kelsey. "But the Amazing Zandra can remove it."

"Are you sure?" Kelsey asked.

Zandra nodded. Then she closed her eyes and started mumbling, rolling her head around in a circle.

Zandra didn't chant like the old gypsy. And she wasn't using the same weird language, either.

When Zandra finally came out of her trance, she took a thick, red marker and made an X on the face of the Fool card. Then she picked up the card and put it into a metal box—which she snapped shut and locked.

"This card will no longer trouble you," Zandra assured Kelsey.

"Is that it?" Kelsey asked. "Is the curse removed?"

"Not yet," Zandra answered. She reached into another box and pulled out a small object. "You must wear this magic amulet for protection."

It didn't look like a magic amulet to Kelsey. It looked like a crystal bead on a string. But Kelsey took it anyway and slipped it over her head.

"Wear the amulet for three days. Never take it off. And at sundown on the third day, the curse will be broken forever."

Kelsey made it through the rest of the day without any problems at all. And she even made it through the night without any creepy nightmares. So by the next morning she was starting to feel a lot better.

But she wasn't going to take any chances. Not until three days had passed. She and Drew stayed around the house the first day, where it was safe. She actually had a lot of fun playing Ping-Pong and board games. She hardly thought about the curse.

By the second day she felt even braver. Brave enough to go to the arcade.

On the very first quarter she dropped on the Wheel of Fortune, she won the video game Drew wanted!

"Wow! Drew, this charm is great!" she said, finger-ing the amulet around her neck. "It's working against the curse—and it's bringing me good luck, too!"

By the time she and Drew headed home, they had armfuls of stuffed animals that Kelsey had won.

On the afternoon of the third day, Kelsey was finally brave enough to go to the beach. The sun was shining. The ocean was warm. And Kelsey was feeling pretty confident that Zandra had removed the curse.

Kelsey and Drew started building a very fancy sand castle.

"Let's build a moat around it," she suggested as she dumped another bucket of sand on the castle.

"Good idea," Drew agreed.

"Here," Kelsey said, waving away an annoying horsefly. "Go fill this bucket with water. I'll start digging."

Drew took the bucket and headed for the water.

Kelsey started digging the trench around the castle.

She glanced around. Their castle was by far the biggest and fanciest one on the beach. She decided to decorate the top with the beautiful, thin, orangy shells her family always called potato-chip shells.

Bzzz. The pesky horsefly landed on Kelsey's leg.

"Ouch!" Kelsey cried as it bit into her skin. "Go away!" Kelsey shooed the fly away again. She noticed a spot of blood where the horsefly had landed.

Bzzz. The fly circled the castle.

53

Drew came back with his first bucket full of water and poured it into the unfinished trench. The sand sucked it all up.

"We're going to need a lot more than that," Kelsey told him.

"Right," Drew agreed. He headed back to the water, bucket in hand.

Kelsey went back to digging the moat when she felt the tickle of tiny legs on the back of her neck.

The horsefly.

She reached back to shoo it away before it could sting her.

It took off, but it continued to buzz around her as she worked on the castle. She jerked her head from side to side as it swooped down at her.

"Just go!" she yelled at it impatiently.

Finally it landed on a shell near the castle, and she continued her work—until she felt a tickle on her leg. Another horsefly.

Before she could swat at that one, a third appeared, landing right on the tip of her nose.

Kelsey jumped up, flailing her arms to get rid of the horseflies.

"Ouch!" she screamed as she felt a sting on the back of her leg. She looked down to see where she'd been bitten, and noticed that there were three horseflies crawling up her thigh.

"Get off!" she shrieked, trying to swat them away.

But they wouldn't leave. In fact, it seemed that as she fought to get rid of them, more of the horrible green-eyed bugs appeared.

"This can't be happening!" Kelsey cried, reaching up to touch her magic amulet. But the amulet was coated with buzzing horseflies. Horseflies that started stinging her hands the moment she touched the charm.

Kelsey began to feel tiny pinpricks all over her body. Hundreds of horseflies flew at her. Hundreds. Stinging her. Over and over again.

She kicked her legs. Waved her arms.

She ran in circles, trying to dodge the ugly insects. But they followed her. They dived at her.

If she didn't get rid of them, every inch of her body would be bitten and bloody.

Their bulging eyes burned brightly as they buzzed around her head. *Buzz. Buzz. Buzz.*

The black cloud of insects circled her face. Closer and closer.

She couldn't breathe.

"I'm going to choke!" Kelsey screamed. "I'm going to choke!"

She swung her head wildly. Her sweat-drenched body heaved in terror.

The flies still surrounded her. Biting deeper and deeper. Burning her flesh.

She tried to shake off the flies, but there were too many of them now. And she fell to the ground, exhausted.

She gasped for breath. She inhaled deeply. Inhaled a mouthful of sand.

Sputtering, gagging, she headed for the ocean. "I'll drown them! I'll drown them!" she screamed.

She raced to the shore, blinded by the horseflies smothering her face.

"Hey! Watch it!" some little kids yelled as she stumbled over their pails and shovels.

Finally she felt the ocean splash beneath her feet. She was about to dive in. Dive under the cool water to soothe her raw, stinging skin.

But someone grabbed her.

"Let go!" she screamed, squirming to break free.

"Where are you going?" Drew asked, holding fast.

"Into the water," she shrieked. "I have to get these horseflies off me."

Drew didn't reply. He didn't have to. His expression told Kelsey everything she needed to know.

There were no horseflies on her.

Not a single one.

Kelsey collapsed into the sand.

The burning and stinging stopped.

"This stupid amulet didn't work," she uttered hopelessly. "Now what am I going to do?"

"Let's go back to the sand castle. We'll think of something," Drew suggested.

He helped her up, and they headed back to their spot on the beach.

"Oh, no!" Kelsey gasped as their sand castle came into view. She pointed a shaky finger at the top of one of its towers.

Drew followed her gaze. And moaned.

"How could this be?" she wailed.

Sticking out of the very top, fluttering in the breeze, was the Fool card—with a bright red X drawn on its face.

12

"**T**he curse isn't broken!" Kelsey screamed. "It's driving me crazy!" Then she snatched up the card and stomped off.

"Hey! Wait up!" Drew yelled. "Where are you going?"

"Back to the Amazing Zandra," she hollered.

Kelsey broke into a run. Drew chased after her. But she didn't stop until she burst through the door of the Amazing Zandra's shack.

Zandra was sitting behind the table with her feet propped up, flipping through a fashion magazine.

She wore a gypsy dress. But it was hiked up so high that Kelsey could see her cutoff jeans underneath it.

And she didn't have long, dark hair anymore. It was

short and blond. The long, dark hair was a wig—and without it, Zandra looked even younger. She didn't look much older than Kelsey.

"You're a fake!" Kelsey shouted at her.

"We've got the card to prove it," Drew added.

Kelsey flung the card down in front of the Amazing Zandra. "Look," she said. "It even has the red X you drew on it. How do you explain that?"

Zandra stared at the card. "Where did you get this?" she asked suspiciously.

"It just appeared," Kelsey told her. "Right after I was attacked by a swarm of horseflies."

"What kind of trick are you two trying to pull on me?" she asked.

"Us?" Kelsey shot back. "You're the one who ripped me off. You said you removed the curse. But you didn't. I was nearly eaten alive by those horseflies! You didn't remove that stupid curse—and this card proves it!"

"That," Zandra declared, "is a different card. The one you brought to me is safely locked inside this box." Then she reached for the metal box and placed it on the table.

"Really?" Kelsey smirked. "Then show it to me."

"No problem," Zandra replied. "I will." She dipped her hand into the pocket of her dress and pulled out the key. She slipped it into the lock and turned it.

Zandra hesitated only for a moment before she lifted the lid.

"Oh, no!" She gasped, staring down into the box. "How can this be?"

Kelsey's eyes were glued to the box. She knew exactly what they would find inside.

Nothing.

Zandra tilted it so that Kelsey and Drew could take a look.

But the box wasn't empty.

And Kelsey shrieked when she spotted what was inside.

13

~~~~

"**O**h, no!" Kelsey cried. "I don't believe this!"

Inside the box was a picture of Kelsey. And there, scrawled across the front, was a big, red X. A big red X right through Kelsey's face.

The Amazing Zandra studied the Fool card that Kelsey had returned. Then she peered into the box at Kelsey's picture. Then back at the card.

"How did you do this?" Zandra demanded.

"How many times do I have to tell you?" Kelsey shouted. "I didn't do anything. The card keeps coming back all by itself. Because I'm under a curse! That's why I paid you ten dollars in the first place. Remember? To take the curse off!"

"Whoa! This is totally freaky," Zandra said. "It sounds to me like you really *are* under a curse."

"That's what we've been telling you all along!" Drew yelled. "Now, can you do anything to help, or not?"

"I don't know," Zandra shrugged. "I think you probably ought to talk to the gypsy who put the curse on you and ask her to remove it."

"But—but," Kelsey sputtered, "I tried that already. The only time I ever saw her was in here. And you told me that was impossible—that there was no other gypsy!"

"I *am* the only gypsy here," Zandra stated. "What was this other gypsy's name? Did she tell you?"

"Yes," Kelsey answered. "But I don't remember what it was. It was something weird."

"Madame something," Drew reminded her. "Madame . . . Madame . . ."

"Valda!" Kelsey blurted out.

"That's it!" Drew agreed. "Madame Valda!"

Zandra's jaw dropped.

"What's wrong?" Kelsey asked.

"That can't be," Zandra said, shaking her head. "Madame Valda. Here? No," she answered her own question. "That just can't be."

"You know who Madame Valda is?" Drew asked.

"Of course," Zandra answered. "Every gypsy in the world knows who Madame Valda is."

"Well, who is she?" Kelsey asked, planting her hands on her hips.

Zandra took a deep breath. "Madame Valda is the most powerful gypsy who ever lived. And the most evil. But you could not possibly have seen Madame Valda," Zandra assured them.

"Why not?" Kelsey wanted to know.

"Because," Zandra said, staring directly into her eyes, "Madame Valda has been dead for more than a hundred years."

14

"**M**adame Valda can't be dead!" Kelsey shouted. "She was sitting right here! Tell her, Drew!"

"She was," Drew insisted.

"Maybe you're thinking of a different Madame Valda," Kelsey told Zandra.

But Zandra shook her head no. "There is only one Madame Valda," she insisted. "And I'm telling you that she has been dead for a really long time."

"But we saw her!" Drew exclaimed. "So that's impossible!"

"Well," Zandra hesitated for a moment. "Not according to some of the old gypsies, it isn't. But I never believed them."

"What do you mean?" Kelsey asked.

"Well, some of the older gypsies believe that Madame Valda can still appear—even after death."

"Yeah, well, you better believe it now," Kelsey declared. "Because I'm telling you—*she was here!*"

"Oh, man." Zandra cringed. "This is tooooo creepy."

"Tell me about it!" Kelsey shot back. "I'm the one who's been cursed by a dead gypsy!"

"So what do we do now?" Drew asked Zandra.

Zandra shrugged. "You've got me."

"Oh, that's just great!" Kelsey huffed. "Just great!"

"Look, don't panic," Zandra told Kelsey. "I have an uncle. He knows all about the old ways. He's the one who told me about Madame Valda. I bet he can help you."

"Where is he?" Drew asked.

"How soon can we see him?" Kelsey added.

"You can see him right now," Zandra answered as she stood up. "Just wait here. I'll go wake him up."

Kelsey and Drew watched Zandra disappear through a curtain of beads that led into a back room.

Kelsey started to pace nervously.

"Do you believe this!" Kelsey was talking more to herself than to Drew. "A dead gypsy put a curse on me! I hope Zandra's uncle is like Super-gypsy or something. Otherwise, I'm doomed."

"You're not doomed," Drew muttered. He didn't sound very convincing.

Just then the beads parted and Zandra headed toward Kelsey and Drew. An old man followed behind.

The man appeared to be as old as Madame Valda herself. Kelsey thought that was a very good sign.

He wore all black. Black pants, black jacket. A worn black leather vest. On a chain around his neck hung a large blue bead.

When Kelsey peered closer, she realized the bead was really a glass eye!

"This is my uncle, Gregor," Zandra said as she approached them.

"It's nice to meet you, Mr. Gregor," Kelsey said as politely as she could. There was no way in the world she was going to insult another gypsy.

Gregor's wrinkled old face showed no expression. He stood as still as a statue and stared at Kelsey. "Zandra tells me that you think you have been cursed by Madame Valda," he finally said.

Gregor spoke in an accent much like Madame Valda's. And Kelsey thought that was an even better sign.

"I don't *think* I've been cursed," Kelsey told Gregor. "I *know* I've been cursed."

Kelsey told Gregor about the Fool card and Madame Valda. She told him all about getting lost, and about the sand crabs. The jellyfish. The horseflies.

Gregor listened without moving. Without even blinking. When she was finished, he said, "I must tell you, this is most unusual."

"No kidding," Drew blurted out. "Especially since Madame Valda is dead!"

"Death is only a bend in the path for someone as powerful as Madame Valda," Gregor told him.

"A what?" Kelsey's eyes opened wide.

"A bend in the path," Zandra repeated. "It means that death can't stop Madame Valda. It just slows her down for a while."

Kelsey turned to Drew in time to see his jaw drop.

"I told you Madame Valda was the most powerful gypsy who ever lived," Zandra said, as if Kelsey needed to be reminded.

"Yes," Gregor agreed. "She was the most powerful gypsy who ever lived. Only she was evil to the bone. And she used her powers in ways that were unthinkable."

"Like how unthinkable?" Kelsey asked, not really wanting to know.

Gregor just shook his head. He didn't answer Kelsey's question. But he continued with his story.

"Madame Valda was so evil that the other gypsies feared her. They feared her for her power. But they also feared that her evil would cause terrible misfortune for all the other gypsies.

"So, secretly, the other gypsies—her own people—decided to kill her. They selected a young boy and a young girl to sneak into her tent and poison her wine."

"Oh, wow!" Zandra exclaimed. Then she sat down and began fanning herself with her fashion magazine.

Gregor went on.

"How the boy and girl managed to trick her—no one knows. But Valda died. Her dead body was thrown into the sea.

"But Valda did not stay in the sea. She has been seen many times and in many places for over one hundred years. And each time she comes back, it is with evil in her heart."

Neither Kelsey nor Drew could speak after Gregor finished his story. But finally Kelsey managed to break the thick silence. "What happened to the boy and girl who poisoned her?"

"Madame Valda cursed them and eventually they went crazy."

"So do you know how to break Madame Valda's curse?" Zandra asked.

Kelsey held her breath, waiting for the answer.

Gregor nodded yes. "But I must warn you, it will not be easy. It will not be easy at all."

Gregor inched closer to Kelsey. She stared at the blue eye dangling from his neck as he spoke in a deep whisper.

"I can remove the curse," he stated. "But removing it will be terrifying—so terrifying that you may think it is *worse* than the curse itself!"

15

Kelsey shivered. She tried to speak in a normal tone, but her voice came out in a squeak. "I have no choice. I want to break the curse."

"Then you must do exactly as I tell you," Gregor said.

"Fine," Kelsey agreed. "Let's just get this over with."

Gregor's wrinkly old face finally cracked into a smile. In fact, he started to laugh. "But you are not ready yet," he told her.

"I'm as ready as I'll ever be," she insisted.

"No," Gregor said. "You are not. There are many things you must do before we can begin. And we can not begin until midnight."

"How come we can't begin right away?" Kelsey asked.

"You must not ask any questions," Gregor told her. "To remove the curse, I must have your trust."

Trust? I don't trust you at all, Kelsey thought. But she knew there was no point in arguing. "Okay," she said. "No questions."

"Good," Gregor declared. "Now listen to me carefully. The first thing you must do is gather up your fears."

"Ask him what that's supposed to mean," Kelsey whispered to Drew—so she wouldn't break Gregor's rules.

"What exactly does that mean?" Drew asked.

Gregor ignored him. "You will bring me a map," he told Kelsey. "And on it you will circle the street where your beach house is located. Understand?"

Kelsey nodded. At least she really did understand that part, even though she had no idea why Gregor needed a map.

"And you will bring me a sand crab," Gregor continued. "One that is still alive."

"Ewwww, gross," Zandra chimed in.

"Hush, Zandra," Gregor scolded. "You must also bring me a big, buzzing horsefly," he continued. "And a lumpy, fat jellyfish. The boy may assist you in finding these things. But you alone must be the one to catch them."

Thinking about touching the crabs and the jellyfish made Kelsey itch all over.

"When you have everything you need, you will come to the gypsy camp. It is under the boardwalk. You must be there by the stroke of midnight," Gregor instructed.

"Don't worry," Kelsey assured him. "We'll be there."

"Good," Gregor said, standing up. "Oh, yes," he added, "there is just one more thing you will need to bring."

"What?" Drew asked.

This time Gregor didn't seem to mind answering Drew's question. "Twenty dollars," he told Drew. "The cost of removing the curse."

And with that, Gregor and Zandra disappeared behind the beads.

Later that afternoon Kelsey started step one of removing the curse: gathering her fears.

The map was easy. She found it in the glove compartment of her mother's car.

Finding a sand crab. That was no problem, either. There were dozens of them crawling around the beach.

But Kelsey couldn't stand to actually touch them. The thought of those creepy, pinchy legs made her

73

skin crawl. So she found a jar in the kitchen and used it to scoop up the icky creature.

Next came the horsefly. She got a second jar for that. Catching that was harder. It wasn't that she couldn't find one. The problem was that there were too many! They swarmed the beach.

Kelsey took a deep breath and ran right into a horde of them.

They landed on her skin. They buzzed in her ears. And they stung her.

When she finally clamped the lid on her jar, she had managed to trap three horseflies.

That left only one more fear.

A jellyfish.

Yuck.

Kelsey swam in the ocean searching for a jellyfish until her lips turned purple and her skin shriveled like a raisin.

But she still didn't have one when her parents called her in for dinner.

By the time she and Drew finished eating and headed back out, the sun was going down. And the beach was totally deserted.

"It's pretty weird being out here all alone," Kelsey commented. Then she thought about how weird it would be going out at midnight—when it was totally black outside. And a shiver ran down her spine.

"Yeah, it is creepy," Drew agreed. "Let's just hope

our parents don't catch us down here. If they do, Madame Valda's curse is going to be the last thing we have to worry about."

But Madame Valda's curse was the *only* thing that Kelsey was worried about. And if she didn't find a jellyfish, she was going to have to worry about it for the rest of her life.

Kelsey headed into the water.

Drew started to follow.

"You stay on the beach," she ordered. "Where you can see me."

"I think I should go with you," Drew argued.

"You can't," Kelsey reminded him. "I have to get the jellyfish myself."

Kelsey started walking out into the ocean. She scanned every inch of the water around her.

No jellyfish—anywhere.

She waded in farther and farther. The water grew deeper. And darker. And colder.

It's really scary out here, she thought as the water rose up to her shoulders.

She turned around to look for Drew. But she couldn't spot him.

She took a few more steps into the ocean—and suddenly the ocean floor dropped beneath her feet.

She plunged down. Down. Down.

Her arms shot up, out of the water. But her head remained beneath the surface.

The current pulled her down—deeper and deeper.

Kelsey struggled to break the water's surface. Struggled to breathe.

She kicked as hard as she could.

Her legs ached. Her lungs burned.

She needed air. She desperately needed air.

Coughing, gasping for breath, she finally burst free.

She gulped the cool night air, filling her lungs. Then she began to swim to shore.

But the water around her grew rough. She lost her rhythm and began to flail.

Concentrate! she told herself. *Concentrate!*

She kicked, hard. Her arms cut through the water.

She swam and swam.

I must be close, she thought, panting. *I must be.*

But when she lifted her head, she froze.

She couldn't see the shore.

She couldn't see anything.

She was lost in a sea of darkness.

16

"**D**rew!" Kelsey screamed. "Drew!" But her cries were drowned by the crashing waves.

Kelsey's eyes darted around her. Trying to focus. Trying to spot a twinkle of light—any clue to show her the way to the shore.

But it was completely dark. So dark that she didn't see the wave forming behind her. The huge wave.

It crested and broke, catching her in a cyclone of foam.

It spun her upside down.

Then it whipped her out of the water.

And she spotted it—the shore. The giant wave had carried her closer to the beach.

"Drew!" Kelsey tried to scream. But a wave washed

over her, and she swallowed a mouthful of the salty sea.

Where was he? Her chest tightened.

Why couldn't she see him? Did he go for help?

Kelsey began to swim again. She was surprised to feel her strokes propel her easily through the water. And as the shore line grew closer, she began to feel better. The tightness in her chest eased.

And then the current changed.

Now it thrashed against her, propelling her sideways.

Directly in the path of a huge stone jetty!

"Nooooooo!" Kelsey screamed at the sight of the jagged rocks.

The waves roared in her ears. Her heart thundered in her chest.

She tried to swim against the force. She cast a glance at the jetty.

She was so close to it now.

So close to being pounded against its pointed, rough rocks.

And then she spotted Drew. Running along the jetty. Jumping from rock to rock.

The waves crashed around her, tossing her body. Tossing her inches from the craggy wall.

"Kelsey!" Drew shouted down. "I'll get help!"

"No!" she cried. "No time!"

A huge wave broke, thrusting her into one of the

78

rocks that jutted out. And a sharp pain shot through her leg.

I can't hold out any longer, Kelsey thought. She could feel the strength seep from her arms. Her legs.

Drew had to help her—now. In another moment she'd be smashed against the jetty.

She lifted her face to call to him one more time.

But he turned—and walked away.

17

The tide pelted Kelsey.

She threw her arms out—to soften the crash against the rough stones.

"Kelsey! Kelsey! Grab this!"

Drew!

He held out a pole—a pole with a red flag on the end. The kind lifeguards use to warn about rough seas.

Kelsey reached out. Stretching.

Grasping—grasping for the pole.

Drew held it out as far as he could.

Her fingertips grazed the end. She almost had it—but a wave broke over her, and the pole slipped from her hand.

She tried again—gripping it tightly this time. And Drew pulled her out of the churning sea.

As she sat on the jetty, gasping for breath, her fingers brushed against something. Something slimy.

She snatched her hand away.

A jellyfish.

She finally had her jellyfish.

"Drew," Kelsey whispered. "Drew, wake up. It's time to go."

Kelsey stood in the doorway of his room. She was wearing black jeans and a black hooded sweatshirt.

Drew sprang out of bed. "I'm up! I'm up!"

He was already dressed, in black jeans and a black sweatshirt too. He even had his sneakers on.

"Come on," Kelsey said as she tugged him out of bed. "It's almost a quarter to twelve. We have to move fast."

"Okay, okay," he muttered. "Do you have everything?"

"Uh-huh," Kelsey told him, patting her backpack. "Right here."

"Is everyone asleep?" he asked.

"Yep." Kelsey headed for the door. "So be quiet."

Kelsey tiptoed down the stairs to the front door. Drew followed.

She opened the door slowly so that it wouldn't

make a sound. Then she and Drew stepped out into the chilly night air.

"Make sure you leave it unlocked," Drew told her. "We need to get back in."

Kelsey nodded as she pulled the door closed behind them. "Let's go!" she cried, and the two started to run.

They didn't stop until they reached the boardwalk. "The gypsy camp must be this way." Kelsey turned to the left.

"Are you sure?" Drew asked.

"Well, it's probably near Gregor's fortunetelling place, right?"

"I guess," Drew said. "You should have asked him."

"No," Kelsey snapped. *"You* should have asked him. *I* wasn't allowed to ask any questions, remember?"

A flicker of light suddenly caught Kelsey's eye.

"Look." She pointed. "I was right!"

"Okay, okay," Drew admitted. "We'd better hurry."

Kelsey glanced at her watch. "Oh, no! It's three minutes to twelve! Let's—"

Drew grabbed Kelsey's arm and tugged her back into the shadows. A dark figure approached.

As it neared, Kelsey could see it was an old gypsy man—dressed in colorful, ragged clothing.

Kelsey stepped forward. She forced a smile. "We're looking for Gregor." Her voice squeaked.

"Then you must come quickly, child," he replied. He was missing almost all of his teeth, and his breath practically knocked Kelsey over. "Gregor is waiting for you. Come." The old man beckoned her with a spindly finger.

Kelsey wasn't so sure she wanted to follow him. But time was running out.

The old man led them under the boardwalk.

Kelsey had never been under the boardwalk. She felt as if she were in a huge cove. It was damp and dark—very dark. She could barely see the wooden planks high above her head.

She took a deep breath to steady her nerves. Her stomach lurched as the stench of dead fish filled her nostrils.

She wanted to turn back. But then she caught sight of a blazing fire up ahead.

As the three moved toward it, she could see gypsies—a crowd of gypsies—sitting in a circle around the crackling flames.

Their colorful clothing and golden jewelry glowed in the fire's light.

Inside the circle stood Gregor. His face flushed from the heat of the flames.

"So, you are here," he said as Kelsey and Drew approached. "Just in time."

All the gypsies rose and turned to stare at Kelsey

83

and Drew. Kelsey didn't like the feeling of all those eyes on her.

"Did you bring everything I commanded?" Gregor asked.

"Yes," Kelsey told him. "I've got them right here."

"Good," Gregor said. "Very good. Come then." He extended his hand. The gypsies parted, allowing Kelsey and Drew to step inside the circle.

Then Gregor clapped his hands together twice— and all the gypsies began to dance.

They danced around the fire, singing an eerie tune—in a language that Kelsey did not understand.

Kelsey didn't know what she was supposed to do. So she stood there and watched. Watched the gypsies whirl around her.

Kelsey recognized Zandra. She was dressed in her gypsy costume, wearing her long, dark wig. And as she danced with the others in the circle, she looked every bit as serious as the rest of them.

When Gregor clapped his hands again, the dancing and singing came to an abrupt stop. And everyone sat.

Gregor reached for an old leather-bound book lying close to the edge of the fire. "May I have all the items, please," he addressed Kelsey.

Kelsey reached into her backpack. First she pulled out the jar with the horseflies. She handed it to Gregor.

He took it without saying a word.

Then she gave him the jar that held the sand crab. He took that, too.

Kelsey had put the jellyfish in a plastic bag. But she still hated touching it. She tossed it over to Gregor quickly.

The last thing Kelsey pulled out of her backpack was the map.

Gregor spread all the items before him.

He turned the tattered pages of his book, searching for the proper chant.

Then he began, chanting in the same strange language Kelsey had heard before. And he rocked back and forth—in a deep, deep trance.

Kelsey wondered what Gregor was saying. But she didn't dare interrupt him.

"Is it over?" she whispered hopefully when Gregor finally stopped his strange song.

"Not yet," he answered. "For the curse to be broken, you must swallow your fears."

"What do you mean?" Kelsey asked.

Gregor nodded at the items on the ground in front of him. "You must swallow your fears," he repeated.

"Are you telling me that I have to eat those things?" Kelsey shrieked.

"Yes," Gregor told her. "It is the only way to break the curse."

18

"**N**o way!" Kelsey said.

Touching sand crabs and jellyfish was disgusting enough. Eating them was out of the question!

"We do not *have* to go on," Gregor declared.

"Yes, yes, we do," Kelsey moaned.

Gregor smiled. "Very well." Then he reached for the jar with the horsefly.

"You're going to do it?" Drew cried.

"I—I have to do it," Kelsey stammered. "I'm not letting that witch beat *me*."

"Are you ready to begin?" Gregor asked.

A hush fell over the bonfire.

Kelsey could hear the sounds of crashing waves in

the distance. The crackling of the flames before her. And the pounding of her heart.

"Yes," Kelsey forced herself to reply. "Only— couldn't we maybe start with the map first?"

Gregor nodded as he placed the jar down and picked up the map.

He tore a piece out of the map, right where Kelsey had circled her street. "Open your mouth."

Kelsey did, and Gregor placed the tiny piece of paper on her tongue. Then he began to chant.

Swallowing the map was really easy. It clung to the back of her throat for a only second. Then she managed to choke it down.

But as Gregor reached for the jar of horseflies, Kelsey's stomach heaved.

When he opened the jar, two of the horseflies escaped. Gregor plucked one of the wings from the horsefly lying in the bottom of the jar and held it out in front of Kelsey.

At least I don't have to swallow the whole thing. She sighed.

She stared at the wing, trying to convince herself that it wasn't going to be as terrible as she thought.

It's just a wing. A tiny, little wing. As harmless as a piece of cellophane.

Kelsey closed her eyes and opened her mouth. And

87

she told herself that that's exactly what it was—a little piece of cellophane.

The moment the wing hit her tongue, she pushed it back toward her throat. Then she swallowed quickly.

She didn't taste a thing. It almost felt like swallowing the skin of a peanut.

Only it wasn't the skin of a peanut. It was the wing of a horsefly. And Kelsey could feel it sticking in her throat. She swallowed and swallowed. But she couldn't make it go down.

She started to choke.

Just as she was about to ask for a glass of water, she saw Gregor reach for the sand crab.

She quickly gathered saliva in her mouth and forced the wing down in one big gulp.

Gregor lifted the crab and removed one of its legs. He dangled it in front of her.

Kelsey shut her lids tightly and tried not to think about it. Then she opened her mouth.

As soon as Gregor placed it on her tongue, she swallowed—hard and fast.

The crab leg scratched her throat as it went down.

Kelsey imagined that it was still alive.

Alive and wriggling back up into her mouth.

Kelsey slammed her hand over her mouth—so she wouldn't throw up.

"You have just one fear left," Gregor stated. Then he pulled out a jeweled knife and sliced off a chunk of the slimy, foul-smelling jellyfish.

The gypsies stared. Silently.

It seemed as if everyone stopped breathing.

Kelsey broke out into a sweat. She wiped her clammy palms on her jeans.

She tried to open her mouth. But she gagged.

"I can't," she cried as she turned her face away from Gregor.

"You must," Gregor told her. "Or the curse will always be with you."

"You can do it, Kelsey," Drew pleaded. "I know you can!"

She shook her head. "No," she told Drew. "I can't."

"Kelsey," Drew replied, "you have to."

Kelsey knew Drew was right. She had to try. "Okay," she said, inhaling deeply. "I'm ready."

Kelsey closed her eyes and held her nose. She opened her mouth. She told herself that if she swallowed it quickly, everything would be okay.

Gregor placed the quivering gunk in her mouth.

It oozed on her tongue.

She forced herself not to think about it. She closed her mouth around the bitter slime.

It tasted salty and fishy. Like eating rotten bait.

89

But the taste wasn't the worst part.

The worst part was how it felt in her mouth.

Slimy—like mucous.

Ooozing and sliding around on her tongue.

Swallow! Kelsey ordered herself. But she gagged again.

Swallow! This time the glob slipped down her throat. Slowly. Kelsey felt her stomach lurch.

She was sure she was going to vomit.

Swallow!

Kelsey had to swallow three times to force the quivering blob down her throat.

She opened her eyes slowly and smiled at Gregor. Drew beamed—as if she had just won an Olympic gold medal.

"You have done very well," Gregor congratulated her. "Very well, indeed. You are a brave girl. And you should be most proud of yourself."

"I am." Kelsey laughed. "I am!"

"You did it, Kelsey!" Drew exclaimed. "You really did it!"

"So, is that it?" Kelsey asked Gregor. "Is the curse all gone now?"

Gregor peered into his magic book. "No," he told Kelsey. "The curse has not yet been broken."

"What else do I have to do?" Kelsey wailed. "What else could there possibly be?"

"You must throw something belonging to Madame Valda into the fire," Gregor told her.

"You never told us that!" Drew yelled.

"Something belonging to Madame Valda!" Kelsey shrieked. "I don't have anything belonging to Madame Valda. I'm doomed," she told Drew. "I'm totally doomed."

19

"**T**here must be another way!" Drew protested.

"No. No other way," Gregor stated.

"Maybe Madame Valda left something in your shack?" Drew turned to Zandra.

"Umm. Let me think. . . ."

"She didn't have anything except that stupid deck of cards," Kelsey interrupted.

"Kelsey!" Drew exclaimed. "That's it! The card! You still have the Fool card! *That* belonged to Madame Valda!"

Kelsey's face lit up. She started rummaging through her backpack to find it. "You're right! We *do* have something that belongs to Madame Valda." She laughed. "And here it is!" Kelsey pulled the Fool card out of her bag.

"I'm not sure this will work," Gregor said, taking the card from Kelsey to examine it.

"What do you mean?" Drew shouted. "Of course it will work. It's Madame Valda's card!"

"Yes, I know," Gregor started to explain. "But the book suggests using an article of clothing or jewelry."

"Yeah," Kelsey snapped. "But we don't have an article of clothing or jewelry. We have a card. Besides, the book doesn't say you *can't* use a card, right?"

"No," Gregor admitted, flipping through the pages. "It doesn't."

"Then this will work!" Drew exclaimed. "This will break the curse!"

Gregor handed the card back to Kelsey. "Yes," he agreed. "This should break the curse!"

The crowd of gypsies cheered.

Kelsey stared down at the card in her hand.

The Fool's haunting face grinned up at her. But this time Kelsey grinned back. She was going to break the curse. Now she was sure of it.

"Approach the fire," Gregor instructed as the crowd fell silent.

Kelsey took a deep breath. Then she stepped up to the flames.

The heat of the fire stung her cheeks—so she backed off, standing just close enough to toss in the card.

"Here goes," she whispered to herself.

She lifted her arm, ready to throw—and the fire began to crackle.

She lowered the card to her side. She glanced around. Then she began again.

But as she raised her arm, the fire's gentle flicker roared to a blaze.

Kelsey jumped back.

The flames soared higher and higher. Hot sparks shot out from their tops.

"What's going on?" she screamed at Gregor.

But Gregor didn't answer. Kelsey could see his face in the glow of the blaze. He looked terrified. He edged back—away from the circle of gypsies.

Kelsey moved in toward the flames.

I have to throw this card in! I have to!

"Hurry!" Drew shouted. "Throw it! Throw it before it's too late!"

Kelsey swung her arm back and—*BOOM!*

The fire exploded in her face. And the flames leaped out—leaped out to grab her!

She screamed and screamed.

And when she finally stopped, she heard a terrifying sound.

A sound she had heard once before.

A sound she would never forget.

The sound of Madame Valda's evil, haunting laugh.

20

Kelsey stared up. Up at the raging fire.

And gasped.

Madame Valda soared up from the center of the flames.

Her fiery body rose high above Kelsey. She loomed over them. Laughing madly.

"Again I face the Fool," she cackled.

Daggers of fire flew from her lips.

"What do we do?" Kelsey cried out to Gregor.

"I . . . I . . . don't know," he stammered, his eyes fixed on the evil gypsy woman.

"What do you mean, you don't know?" Kelsey screamed.

"He doesn't know because he is a fake!" Madame

Valda bellowed. "How can you believe in this gypsy clown—and not believe in Madame Valda!"

Kelsey whirled to face Gregor. He inched back again—farther and farther from the old woman.

"He is no gypsy!" Madame Valda roared. "He has no powers! There is nothing in his stupid, little magic book to help you."

Then Madame Valda pointed her finger at Kelsey. "Fool!" she cried.

A firebolt shot out from her fingertip—and the gypsies began to scatter.

"They are frauds," Madame Valda spat. "All of them. There is not one true gypsy among them."

As she spoke, she turned her hands upward. Pillars of black smoke burst from her palms.

"I'm out of here!" Zandra screamed and took off down the beach.

Madame Valda cackled at the sight.

"Come on, Kelsey." Drew grabbed Kelsey's arm. "Let's go!"

"I can't," Kelsey groaned. "If I don't face her now, I'll be under this curse forever."

Madame Valda laughed her evil laugh. "You are going to pay for angering Madame Valda yet again." Her eyes burned right through Kelsey. "Not only does this Fool insult me once, she enlists the help of more fools to insult me again!"

Kelsey spun around to face the other gypsies. But

no one remained. They had abandoned her—left her alone to fight the hideous witch.

"Did you really think you could get rid of my curse so easily?" Madame Valda crooned. "Well, think again! You will never get rid of it! Never!"

Madame Valda's laughter echoed through the night. Her hot red eyes bore into Kelsey.

"Kelsey!" Drew shouted. "Throw the card into the fire!"

"Go ahead, Fool," Madame Valda taunted. "Try to burn it! Try!"

"Stop calling me Fool!" Kelsey cried. Then she inched forward, her eyes glued to the ugly gypsy.

"Come, Kelsey." Madame Valda beckoned with a fiery finger. "Come closer to the flame!"

Kelsey stepped forward—and Madame Valda hurled a fireball at her feet.

Kelsey leaped away and fell.

"Come, Kelsey." Madame Valda laughed. "You can do it!"

"Kelsey!" Drew screamed. "Are you okay?"

Kelsey nodded, jumping to her feet.

"I have to try again!"

Kelsey glanced up at Madame Valda. The evil gypsy's eyes were closed!

"Throw it!" Drew screamed. "Throw it now!"

She must be tired, Kelsey thought.

"Now!" Drew screamed.

Kelsey swung her arm and hurled the card into the fire.

"Yes!" Drew's shouts echoed as Kelsey watched the card sail straight for the flames.

And then she felt it.

A strong wind against her face.

"Nooooo!" she shrieked as the card flew from the fire.

It rode the burst of hot air Madame Valda released from her chest.

Kelsey gaped in horror as her only hope blew away.

21

~~~

The Fool card soared past Kelsey.

Way above her head.

Way out of her reach.

Out—out toward the beach.

"Oh, no!" Kelsey cried. "It's headed for the ocean!"
Kelsey and Drew tore down the beach after the
fluttering card. It appeared as a dim white speck as it
floated out—out to sea.

Madame Valda's laughter cut through the air, but
Kelsey didn't turn back. She ran. Ran for her life.

"I can get it! I've got to!"

The beach was pitch black. Kelsey wanted to look
down—to see where she was running. But she didn't.

She trained her eyes on the card. She could lose sight of it in a blink.

She ran faster. Faster.

But suddenly she felt heat at her back.

"She's chasing us!" Drew screamed.

Kelsey turned—and saw a huge ball of fire streak through the sky. It swooped down—and spun around her.

She stared in terror as Madame Valda soared up from the fireball's center. Dripping fire.

The flames licked at Kelsey's legs . . . arms . . . hair.

She threw her arms over her head and screamed.

"There is no way to escape me, Fool." Madame Valda's fiery breath hit the back of Kelsey's neck. "No way at all."

The card! Kelsey had lost sight of the card!

She jerked her head around. There it was! Dipping down—right in front of her.

Kelsey sprang up for it. And just as her finger brushed its tip, the gypsy's hot breath blew it away.

"Nooooo!" Kelsey screamed. "Nooooo!"

The card flipped and spun in the air.

Kelsey leaped for it.

The evil gypsy blew it again—blew it from her grasp.

"To the sea!" Madame Valda cackled. "To the beautiful *black* sea!"

The card swirled in front of Kelsey. It fluttered down in front of her face. Then rose up sharply.

Kelsey lunged for it. But it whirled around her.

Taunting her.

Then it sailed out to the shore.

Kelsey lunged again. Plunging in the cold, inky water.

"Say goodbye, you little fool!" Madame Valda shrieked. Then she threw her head back and roared with laughter.

And just as she did, Kelsey snatched the card from the air—and thrust it directly in the center of Madame Valda's flaming body!

"Here's your card back, Madame Valda!" Kelsey spat.

"Nooooooo!"

Madame Valda's screams rang out through the night. Her fiery form exploded in an enormous burst of light. And tore through the blackened sky.

Kelsey smiled as she watched the fire fade—as Madame Valda's features began to melt.

Her fiery figure shriveled up—smaller and smaller.

And then she disappeared in a puff of smoke.

22

"**N**o! No! Noooo!" Kelsey screamed when she heard the explosion.

"I won!" Drew shouted. "I won!"

Kelsey glared at the clown she had been aiming at. Its inflated balloon head bobbed from side to side.

She set down her water pistol, defeated. "Only because I let you win," she shot back.

Drew just laughed as the carnival barker handed him his prize—a giant pretzel. He broke it in two and gave her half.

"Thanks." She smiled. "What should we do next?"

"Let's go through the haunted house again," he suggested. "The Shadyside Carnival has the best haunted house!"

"That's because Shadyside is the best haunted town," Kelsey joked.

"I'm glad we made it back from the beach in time for the carnival," Drew said as the two headed for the haunted house ride.

"I'm glad we made it back at all," Kelsey replied.

"Oh, brother!" Drew pointed up ahead. "Look at that line!"

The line for the haunted house curved all the way around the ride twice.

"We'll be here forever," Kelsey complained. "Let's find something else to do."

"Like what?" Drew asked. Then he gasped.

"What?" Kelsey cried.

"Look!" He pointed to a sign that read "Gypsy Fortuneteller."

"That?" She laughed. "That's nothing. It's just a mechanical fortuneteller inside a glass box. Come on, I'll show you."

Drew hesitated.

"Come on!" she said again, tugging him over to the glass box.

As they neared it, a little girl slipped a quarter into the slot and waited for the mechanical fortuneteller to whirl around and tell her fortune.

She waited. And waited. And waited.

"This stupid thing is broken," the little girl com-

104

plained, kicking the box. Then she gave up and walked away.

"See?" Kelsey said. "Nothing to be afraid of."

Drew stared at the box. "Just a machine," he said, breathing a sigh of relief.

Then she and Drew turned and walked away.

"Not afraid?" a voice called after them.

They stopped.

"Fool! Fool! Fool!" The voice cackled now. "Only a fool is not afraid!"

Are you ready for another walk
down Fear Street?
Turn the page for a terrifying
sneak preview.

FRIGHT KNIGHT

Coming mid-March 1996

The thrills and chills begin when Mike and Carly help their dad unpack a suit of armor—a display for his latest project, the Museum of History's Mysteries. Mike knows Sir Thomas Barlayne was the most evil knight that ever lived. And that his armor is supposed to be haunted! Those horrible stories of the evil knight's ghost can't be true . . . Can they?

Dad and Mr. Spellman lifted the lid off the crate. I scooted forward. I held my breath. Carly stood right next to me.

We all leaned over and peered inside.

All I saw was piles and piles of shredded newspaper.

"It's paper." Carly sounded as disappointed as I felt.

Dad grinned. "Not just paper, Carly," he said. "Go ahead. Reach in there and see what you can find."

"Me?" Carly squeaked.

"Are you afraid?" Dad asked.

"No way," she said. I could tell she was scared silly, but acting like everything was cool.

The long crate suddenly reminded me of a coffin. I wondered if Carly had the same idea too.

Her mouth twitched. She pushed up a sleeve of her blue sweater. She reached into the crate. Her arm disappeared into the mountains of paper shreds.

The paper rustled as she felt around for something solid. I saw her lean over and reach in even deeper.

"I think I feel something," she told us.

Then she screamed.

"It's got me! It's grabbed me! Help!"

I watched Carly try and try again to yank her arm out.

But something . . . or someone . . . had grabbed her.

And it wouldn't let go.

Carly tugged and squirmed. Her face turned red. Dad and Mr. Spellman started digging. Shredded newspaper flew in all directions.

"Hold on now, honey," Dad said.

"Hurry! It's got me," she wailed.

She was out of control. Even I felt sorry for her. Well, almost.

Dad pulled up her arm. The fingers of a metal hand were wrapped around Carly's wrist.

"Well, would you look at this," Dad said. He

laughed. The metal hand was attached to a long metal arm.

"Your bracelet got caught," Dad said. "Hold still. I'll have you unhooked in a second." He pried the metal fingers open one by one. Carly snatched back her hand.

The metal hand and arm dropped back into the crate with a clunk.

"Stupid armor," Carly grumbled. She looked down at her wrist, rubbing it.

I looked over my shoulder at Mr. Spellman. I rolled my eyes. He rolled his too.

Dad reached into the next box and pulled out another piece. "Now look at this," he said.

Smiling, Dad held up a helmet. The last rays of the setting sun glinted on the metal, turning it glowing red. Hot. Fiery.

My mouth fell open. I didn't even realize I was holding my breath till I let it go. "Cool! It's so cool."

Then Dad handed the helmet to me. Just looking at the helmet was nothing compared to touching it.

I ran my hands over the armor. It felt heavier than I thought it would. And not cold. Not like metal should be. It felt warm. The way it would be if somebody had just taken it off.

A shiver crawled up my back. I cradled the helmet in my arms. Dad pulled a metal shin guard out of the crate and set it on the floor. A metal foot guard came next.

Dad's eyes gleamed. He reached into the pile of shredded paper for another piece of the armor. "This is it! Our chance at fame and fortune. This is going to be the best and the spookiest exhibit anyone has ever seen. On Fear Street or anywhere else. People will come from all over the world to see it and—"

His words stopped suddenly. His sandy-colored eyebrows drew together as he frowned. He kept moving his hand around under the shredded paper. He felt around for something way down at the bottom of the crate.

"What's this?" Dad pulled his arm out. He held up something bright and shiny. The strange round object dangled at the end of a long, golden chain.

It looked like a giant marble, but weirder looking than any marble I had ever seen.

Inside the marble strange blue smoke swirled and twisted. Dark blue. Light blue. Sparkling silvery flecks whirled slowly around in the smoke, like tiny shooting stars.

I grabbed for it.

So did Carly.

So did Mr. Spellman.

I got there first.

"Slower than snails!" I grinned at them, the pendant in my hands. "This must be my special surprise from Uncle Basil!" I slipped the chain over my neck before anybody else had a chance to touch it. I stared down at the pendant dangling against my white T-shirt. "Gee—it looks cool, doesn't it?"

Dad agreed. So did Carly. She sounded jealous. That made me like the pendant even more.

Mr. Spellman stepped forward. "If you ask me," he said, looking at the pendant, "it looks positively magical."

"Yeah, it does sort of, doesn't it?" I nodded.

A magic pendant.

It was the best surprise I'd had since Dad took us to New York City last year to buy a new mummy.

We all watched as Dad finished unpacking the crate. We gathered up the armor and took it into the front hall.

Mr. Spellman and I handed Dad the pieces.

Piece by piece, he slowly put Sir Thomas together.

Carly stood by, holding our cat in her arms. I could tell she didn't want to touch the armor.

When he finished, we all stood back and took a good look.

Sir Thomas's armor could have easily fit my favorite pro wrestler, Hulk Hooligan. The shoulders were about a yard wide. The legs were round and solid. They reminded me of small tree trunks. About three of me could have hidden behind the breastplate, no problem.

I thought about all the stories in all my books about castles and knights.

"Awesome!" I let out the word at the end of a sigh.

"He does look awesome, doesn't he?" Mr. Spellman clapped me on the back.

Dad smiled. "Now all we have to do is keep our fingers crossed. If we're lucky, this old pile of metal really is haunted. And that will bring the customers running!"

The phone rang and Dad went to answer it. Mr. Spellman hurried out too. He said he had some work to do down in the wax museum. After they left, Carly edged up real close to me.

"What do you think, Mikey?" She always called me Mikey when she was trying to make me mad. "Are you scared the armor might really be haunted?"

"The only thing I'm scared of is your ugly face!" I gave her a plalyful punch on the arm. I dashed out of the room and up the stairs.

It was my turn to start dinner. I knew exactly what I was going to make—macaroni and cheese, the food Carly hated more than anything in the whole wide world.

It was Carly's turn to do the dishes. I made sure I cooked the macaroni and cheese just a little too long. She had to scrape all the hard pieces off the bottom of the pot. While she was doing that and grumbling to herself, I hurried to my room.

I still had an end-of-the-year school project to do about polar bears. I had to read the report to my class tomorrow. Also my favorite TV show, *Scream Theater*, was on at nine.

I got my homework done, but I never got a chance to watch *Scream Theater*. It had been a big day. I was beat.

I brushed my teeth, pulled on my pajamas and fell into bed.

But I kept my pendant on. Stretched out in bed, I held it up in front of my face. I watched the curling blue smoke glimmer in the moonlight that slipped through my window.

I got this weird feeling that the smoke was hiding something. Something really great. I tried to get a closer look. But the more I looked, the more the color swirled.

I fell asleep before I knew it.

Thump. Thump.

I was dreaming about something. I couldn't remember what. I thought it had something to do with polar bears. And blue marbles. And knights in shining armor.

Thump. Thump.

There it was again.

I opened my eyes and listened.

Thump. Thump.

Definitely not part of my dream.

I sat up and held my breath.

Thump. Thump.

It came from downstairs.

Thump. Thump.

I swung my legs over the side of the bed. I sat with my head tilted, listening harder.

Thump. Thump.

I couldn't think of anything down in the museum that made that kind of noise.

At least, not before tonight.

Thump. Thump.

I stood up. My legs felt a little rubbery.

Only one thing could be making the noise.

The armor.

Thump. Thump.

I gulped and hurried downstairs. The kitchen was right under my room. The closer I got to it, the louder the sound got.

Thump. Thump.

I gazed down at my pendant. The swirling blue smoke pulsed to the rhythm of the sounds.

Thump. Thump.

At the door to the kitchen, I stopped. I gulped for air, the way I do in gym class when Mr. Sirk, our PE teacher, makes us run extra laps.

This was it! My chance to catch a ghost in action. My chance to prove that the armor really was haunted!

Thump. Thump.

I took a deep breath. I pushed open the kitchen door.

Thump. Thump.

I took a couple of shaky steps inside.

Thump. Thump.

I squinted into the dark. Then I saw it.

It was hideous. Creepy. Disgusting.

I couldn't help it. I had to scream.

About R. L. Stine

R. L. Stine, the creator of *Ghosts of Fear Street,* has written almost 100 scary novels for kids. The *Ghosts of Fear Street* series, like the *Fear Street* series, takes place in Shadyside and centers on the scary events that happen to people on Fear Street.

When he isn't writing, R. L. Stine likes to play pinball on his very own pinball machine, and explore New York City with his wife, Jane, and fifteen-year-old son, Matt.

Is The Roller Coaster Really Haunted?

THE BEAST

❏ 88055-1/$3.99

It Was An Awsome Ride—Through Time!

THE BEAST 2

❏ 52951-X/$3.99

A MINSTREL® BOOK

Published by Pocket Books